D0568990

I Am Me!

ALEXA BRANDENBERG

Red Wagon Books
Harcourt Brace & Company
San Diego   New York   London

Red Wagon Books is a trademark of Harcourt Brace & Company.

Library of Congress Cataloging-in-Publication Data
Brandenberg, Alexa.
I am me!/Alexa Brandenberg.
p.   cm.
"Red Wagon Books."
Summary: Children imagine their future careers as a
fireman, an archaeologist, a chef, and others.
ISBN 0-15-200974-4
[1. Occupations—Fiction.]   I. Title.
PZ7.B73625Iaad   1996
[E]—dc20   95-17110

First edition
A C E F D B

Printed in Singapore

To my parents
(because without them I could not be me!)
and to Jeff,
for his unshaking optimism

When I
grow up
I want
to be

a fireman

a carpenter

an archaeologist

a ballerina

a librarian

a doctor

an artist

a violinist

and a chef.

But for now
I am
ME,

and I will climb

hammer

dig

dance

read

bandage

paint

practice

and bake!

What will you do?